Also in the series

The Secret Lives of Unicorns

The Secret Lives of Mermaids

For my family, forever sharing their laughter, truth and fire.
- Zoya Agnis

For all the people in my life who give me wings and armour.
- Alexander Utkin

First edition published in 2021 by Flying Eye Books,
an imprint of Nobrow Ltd. 27 Westgate Street, London, E8 3RL.

1 3 5 7 9 10 8 6 4 2

Published in the US by Nobrow (US) Inc.
Printed in Latvia on FSC® certified paper.

ISBN: 978-1-83874-047-4
www.flyingeyebooks.com

The Secret Lives of DRAGONS

Professor Zoya Agnis Alexander Utkin

FLYING EYE BOOKS
London | Los Angeles

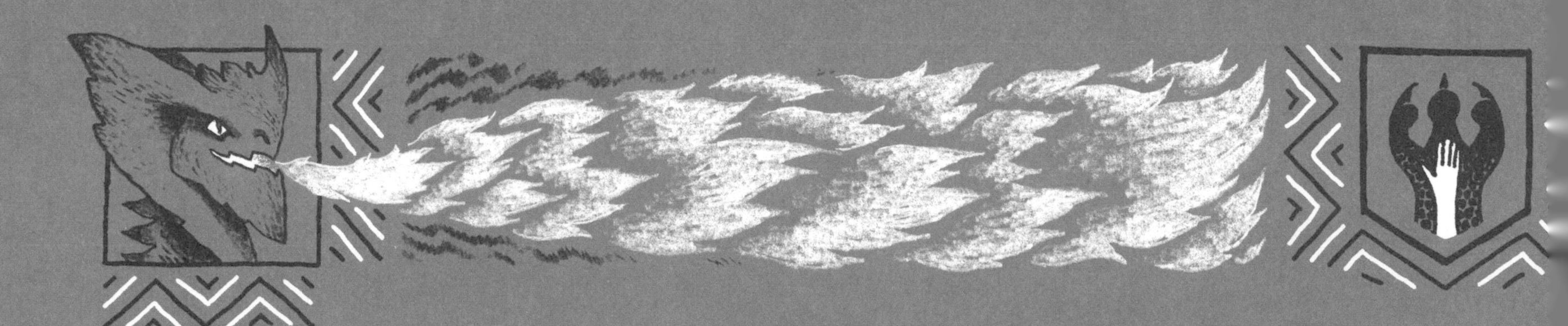

CONTENTS

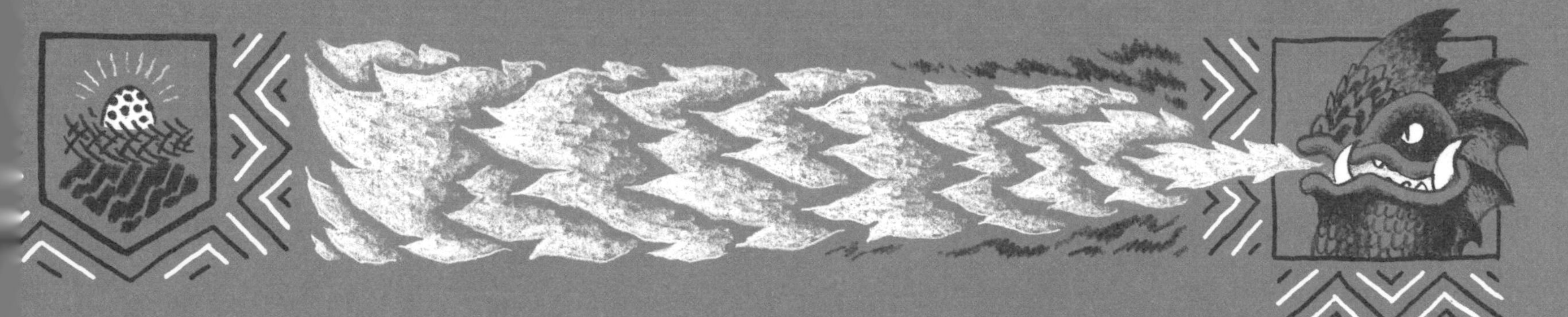

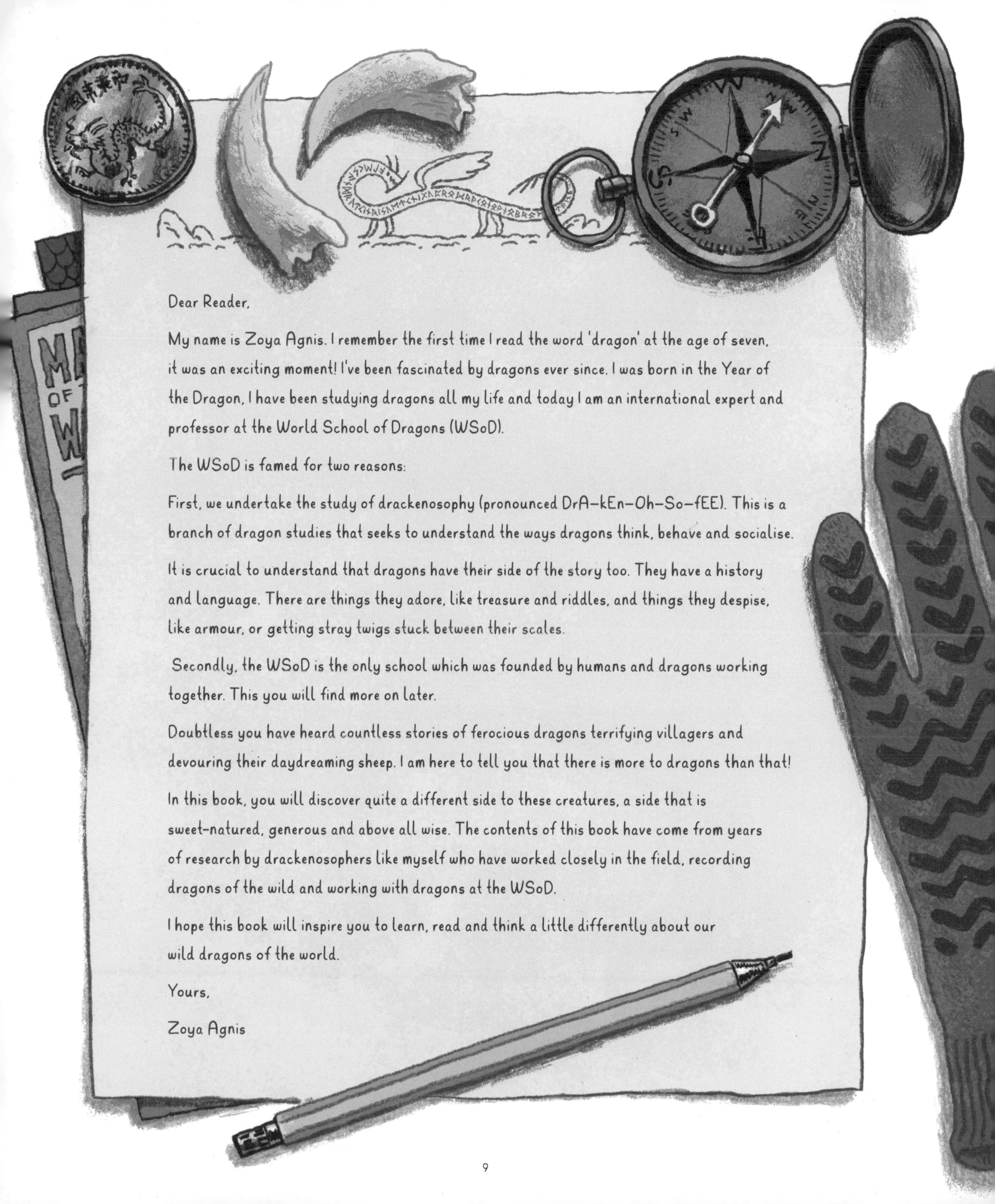

Dear Reader,

My name is Zoya Agnis. I remember the first time I read the word 'dragon' at the age of seven, it was an exciting moment! I've been fascinated by dragons ever since. I was born in the Year of the Dragon, I have been studying dragons all my life and today I am an international expert and professor at the World School of Dragons (WSoD).

The WSoD is famed for two reasons:

First, we undertake the study of drackenosophy (pronounced DrA–kEn–Oh–So–fEE). This is a branch of dragon studies that seeks to understand the ways dragons think, behave and socialise.

It is crucial to understand that dragons have their side of the story too. They have a history and language. There are things they adore, like treasure and riddles, and things they despise, like armour, or getting stray twigs stuck between their scales.

Secondly, the WSoD is the only school which was founded by humans and dragons working together. This you will find more on later.

Doubtless you have heard countless stories of ferocious dragons terrifying villagers and devouring their daydreaming sheep. I am here to tell you that there is more to dragons than that!

In this book, you will discover quite a different side to these creatures, a side that is sweet-natured, generous and above all wise. The contents of this book have come from years of research by drackenosophers like myself who have worked closely in the field, recording dragons of the wild and working with dragons at the WSoD.

I hope this book will inspire you to learn, read and think a little differently about our wild dragons of the world.

Yours,

Zoya Agnis

Part I

WHAT IS A DRAGON?

Dragons are fire-breathing, scaly animals with incredible eyesight. In fact, the name 'dragon' is related to the Greek word 'dérkesthai', which means 'to see clearly'. This not only applies to their sight, but their formidable intellect! Modern dragons are descendants of ancient reptilian animals. They lay eggs, they are covered in an armour of shimmering scales and scutes (thick bony plates) and they are vertebrates (they have a spine), just like many of the reptiles we already know so well.

Modern dragons are a spectacular sight to behold! Although many exist across the globe, they are tough to spot out in the wild. The best way to catch a glimpse is to arm yourself with as much research as possible before going out to explore. So let's find out more about them, starting 230 million years ago with their evolution...

Evolution of Dragons

Evolution is the process of gradual change over a very long period of time. All creatures on Earth have evolved, and today they may look very different from their ancestors long ago. Dragons are no different. They started as small, insect-eating dinosaurs and changed slowly over millions of years to become the extraordinary creatures we know today.

Archosauricadrako

Triassic: 245–208 mya✦

The oldest dragon ancestor was an insect-eating animal with a spiny sail along its back. It walked on four short legs and lived near water. Its fire wasn't powerful, but it was an incredibly effective defence against larger dinosaurs.

✦Million years ago

Boggoradrake

Jurassic: 208–144 mya

Bigger, stronger and armoured, the Boggoradrake was the scourge of rivers, lakes and swamps. Its scales were thick for optimal protection and its talons grew sharp to pick at barnacles and slash at large fish.

Dracken flighticus

Cretaceous: 144–66.4 mya

The winged dragon takes flight! The wings developed from the sail that once helped it swim in waters. The winged dragons were smaller than the land dragons, which helped them take to the air. Many dragon species started to evolve from Dracken flighticus.

Dracken mindus

Eocene: 66.4–33.9 mya

Following the K-T extinction✦✦, only six true species of dragon remained. Their heads grew larger as they gained more intelligence and their eyes became sharper. Eventually, they spread across the globe, seeking safe places to settle.

Modern dragons

Oligocene: 33.9 mya–today

Each of the six dragon families (or species) have adapted to suit a particular environment, including mountains, deserts and water. During the last 30 million years, these intelligent creatures have created their own language and well-ordered societies.

✦✦Caused by the deadly comet that struck Earth and wiped out almost all plants and animals, including most dinosaurs

Anatomy

Dragons are uniquely built to attack, defend, surprise and outwit. They have adapted superbly to survive in the different environments that they inhabit, yet all dragons share similar anatomical features across the six families.

Scales

Dragons are covered in thick, impenetrable armour made of scales, formed in a regular pattern. There are only two unshielded spots, on either side of the chest, where the scales fan out as they move.

Talons

These sharp claws are perfectly made to cling to craggy surfaces and are razor-sharp to rip at meat, too. Dragons have three to five talons on each limb. Their wings are also tipped with talon-like 'fingers', which are sharp hooks used for extra grip and protection.

Wings

The wings of a dragon are famously large and strong. The largest can stretch to almost 20 metres (65 feet) wide. They are usually tipped with one or more 'fingers' (see talons), and are made of thick, leathery skin. All of the bones inside them are hollow so that the wings are light enough for the dragon to fly easily, no matter the size or shape.

Tail

The tails are strong and muscular to help them balance. Even the smallest dragon can whip and slash them through the air like a knife. Tail shapes vary: some have forked ends while others taper out into a spike.

Horns

The largest dragon horn on record is one metre (3 feet) long. Horns are used to spear enemies or dig out lairs from rock and earth. They come in a variety of shapes and sizes. They can be small, round and stubby for cracking through ice and rock, or thin and needle-like to swiftly kill prey.

Eyes

Dragons are famed for their superior eyesight. They can spot movement or catch the glint of metal up to 3.2 km (2 miles) away, both to the sides and straight ahead. They also have an extra eyelid which sweeps sideways every few seconds to remove dirt.

Teeth

These can be as long as a human forearm. Whilst the fang itself is not venomous, the gums excrete a toxic saliva that can kill. The teeth form two rows on the bottom and top, with two large incisors resting over the bottom lip.

Digestive System

Dragons are not fussy with their diets. They will eat sheep, ox, horse, goat, pig, zebra, lion, bear and even hippo. For a snack they delight in gobbling up a whole chicken like popcorn, toasted feathers too. Contrary to popular belief, they do not like the taste of humans!

Breathing Fire

A dragon creates fire by mixing two chemicals that it naturally produces in its body. The first is a stinky, eggy gas called 'belchium gastate' which grows in the gut and belly. The second is the noxious 'stenchic expelorium', which is excreted from the glands in the mouth and snout, and smells a lot like petrol. On their own, these gases are mildly poisonous but not dangerous. It's only when they are mixed together that they create... FIRE!

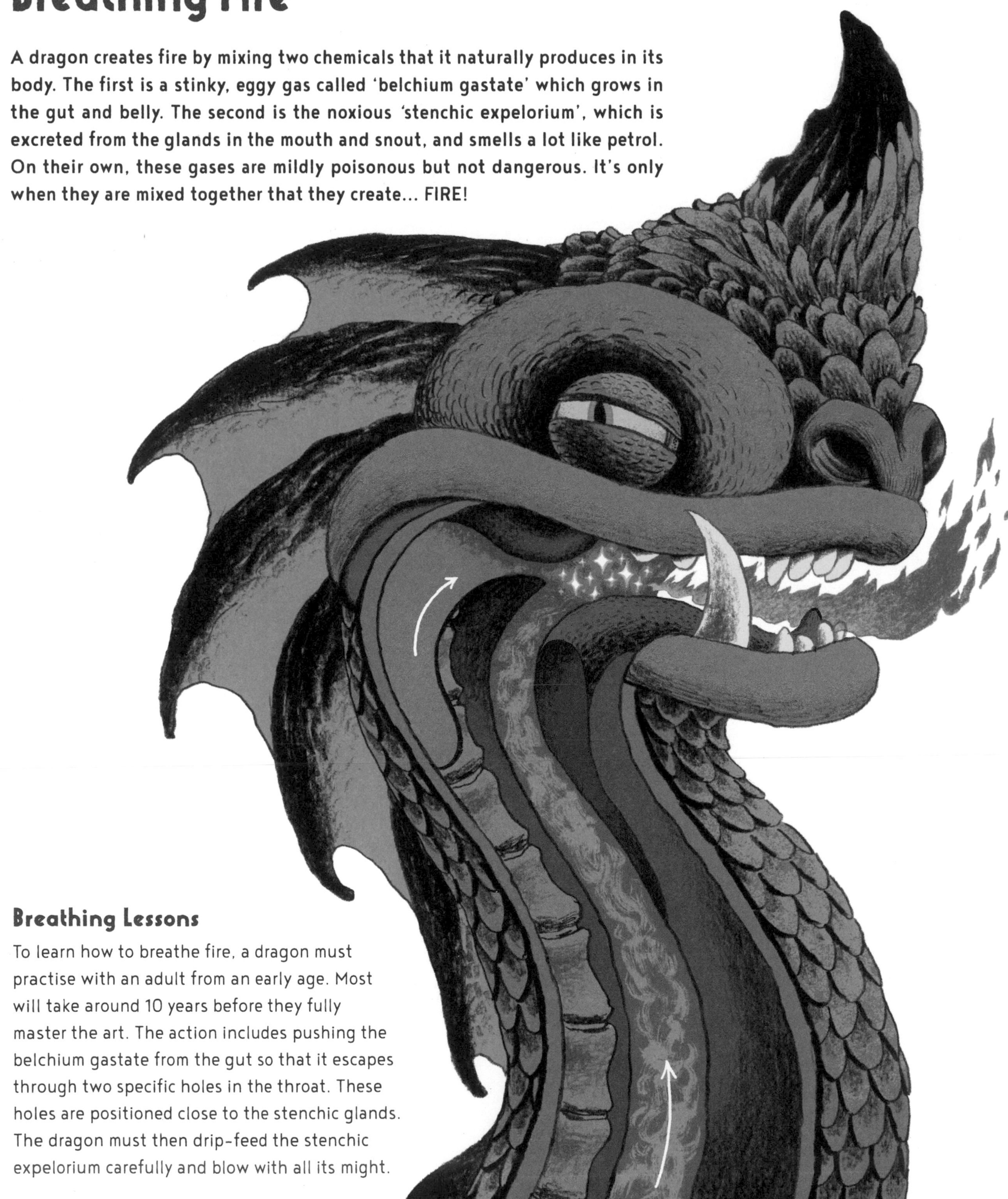

Breathing Lessons

To learn how to breathe fire, a dragon must practise with an adult from an early age. Most will take around 10 years before they fully master the art. The action includes pushing the belchium gastate from the gut so that it escapes through two specific holes in the throat. These holes are positioned close to the stenchic glands. The dragon must then drip-feed the stenchic expelorium carefully and blow with all its might.

Fire and Feelings

Fire colour is not always a deep orange. In dragons it can change according to how they feel.

Orange: the colour of flames used to attack

Purple: shows a dragon is feeling a deep sadness

Pink: shows hope and joy

Green: excited dragons spit out emerald flames

Blue: used when feeling mischievous

Black: a low, simmering fire is used to warm dragon eggs

Random Emissions

Fire is not a dragon's first choice for defence or attack, but it will use fire when offended. Drackenosophers have noted that random blasts of flame will be sent out as a warning before a dragon fully releases the fire. In addition, a dragon must occasionally burp to let out gases in its stomach. Do not mistake a dragon releasing wind for an angry blast!

Flight

A dragon in flight sweeps through the air with delightful grace. It spirals and crashes into clouds then – pop! The dragon bursts through the other side, flicking small trails of water vapour off its tail as it soars into the sky. Launching into the air is a tricky manoeuvre for animals as large as dragons. They all use the same method to get airborne, but once they're up their flight patterns are not the easiest thing to monitor! One incredible feature that drackenosophers have noted is that groups of dragons fly in strict formation.

Dragons need to gallop for a few minutes in order to get enough momentum to take off.

Larger flying dragons live closer to the oceans or near windy crevasses where they use strong gales and updraughts to help them glide in the air. The use of winds to glide high up is called 'volplaning'.

How Dragons Fly

1. Take off: Pulling themselves forward onto their limbs, they thunder across the ground to gain speed. Their wings pull forward and their powerful legs and forearms push off the ground with monumental force.

2. Catapulting: Up into the air, they spin like a rocket, twisting as they go until they reach cloud level.

3. Diving: Wings fold back close to the body, the dragon plunges towards the ground like a rocket. Their eyes are squeezed to the thinnest slits, and their tail is pulled back into a sharp line.

4. Landing: The most common landing technique is to gently circle back down to the ground. The wings are spread in order to slow their speed as they approach land.

As dragons flap their wings from above, they can push the clouds down to create ground-hugging 'dragon fog', a telltale sign that a dragon is nearby.

Birth and Death

An animal's life can be measured in stages, from when they are born until the time they die. This is the life cycle. Dragons have a very long life, and so from a young age they learn how to grow strong and keep themselves busy.

Eggs and Newborns

Dragons hatch from eggs. These are about the size of a football and vary in colour depending on the dragon species. A newly-hatched baby can be anything between 30 and 40 cm (12 and 16 inches) long, about the same size as a cat. In the first few weeks, their eyes are still sealed shut so they rely on their parents to take care of them. They are born with a soft down, which they quickly lose.

Young Dragons

Between the ages of one and ten, dragon children learn to fly and properly master the art of fire-breathing. They are still very vulnerable so tend to stay close to their parents during this time. Dragon families live in lairs, which are fiercely guarded by the parents. The day a young dragon moves out of the nest is a big day for the family! The event is marked with a huge celebration and plenty of gift-giving.

Mature Dragons

When they are old enough, many dragons set out to find a partner to share their life with. Their extravagant mating rituals include dancing, singing and solving their most complicated riddles together. Dragons can be quite the performers when they want to be! Lair-building is also a good way to show off. The cosier and more secret the lair, the more impressive the dragon.

Older Dragons

Ageing wears down a dragon's bones so the older ones tend to sleep long hours. When awake, they pass the time by blowing smoke rings, telling stories and grooming each other. When a dragon dies, a fire ceremony is performed. The family come together to sing a sweet and soulful song, after which they let out a fiery burst to let the old dragon burn into the earth. The oldest recorded dragon was 500 years old.

Part II

DRAGONS OF THE WORLD

Dragons are classed into six main species – although dragons tend to call themselves the 'Six Great Families'. The six different species are not separated by country, as the notion of a country does not mean much to a dragon. Instead, where they choose to live depends on the type of climate or land they prefer. In Britain, for example, you can find one species in a mountain lair, while another will live in the marshlands below.

Families tend to live together in small neighbourhoods (although small is a matter of opinion, a dragon's home may look as large as a castle to us!). This chapter will tell you where to find the different dragons, what makes them distinct from each other and some of the fascinating characteristics that they are famous for.

The Prajnath Family

Dragons of the Prajnath family are glorious to spot in the wild. Their brightly coloured scales are framed by plumes of fine, sharp hair. These are all toxic so it is best not to get too close. They live in mountainous regions, dipping through crystal lakes and taking flight by gliding on currents of mountain air. They enjoy the dark and are the most secretive of dragons. Consider yourself lucky indeed if you come across one of these!

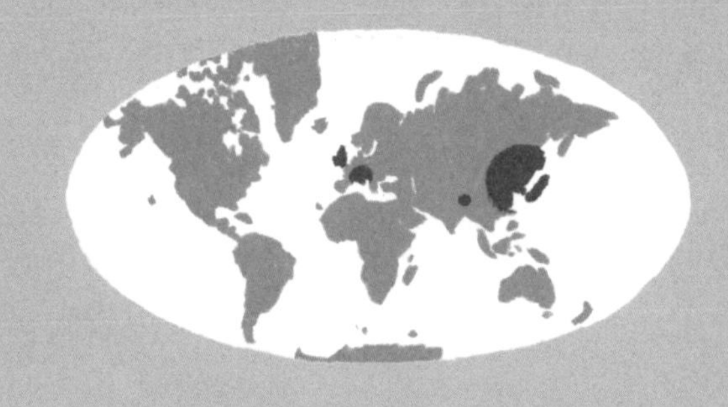

Terrain: Mountains and lakes

Sightings: Bhutan, China, Japan, Scotland and Swiss Alps

Colour: Gold, green, red, silver or yellow

Size: 24 metres / 80 feet

The Wise Word Keeper

The Prajnath family are famed for talking almost completely in riddles! They are the keepers of the dragon language, and of vast amounts of knowledge. The oldest 'Word Keeper' lives in the green mountains of Guilin in China where the peaks are circled by clouds. Her age has turned her golden mane into silver, marking her wisdom among the dragons. Anyone coming to seek her help will be faced with a question: 'I am full of leaves but have no roots, what am I?' (the answer: a book!) Those that can answer correctly will have their own questions answered. The famous advice she gives to anyone who visits her is 'wisdom is how you choose to use your power.'

The Vedanith Family

The rarest and perhaps the most spectacular of dragons is the feathered Vedanith. Their wings are covered in stiff, waxy plumage, harder than a bird's feather but just as sleek and beautiful. These exquisite dragons are mostly found in the Andes of South America and the volcanic peaks of Central America. They bask in the fire that comes from the Earth's belly, and they flap their wings like colossal fans if they get too hot. The Vedanith's snout has evolved to block the smell of sulphur (very similar to rotten eggs) that spews from volcanoes. They have a distinctive feathery mane, which fans out when they are angry.

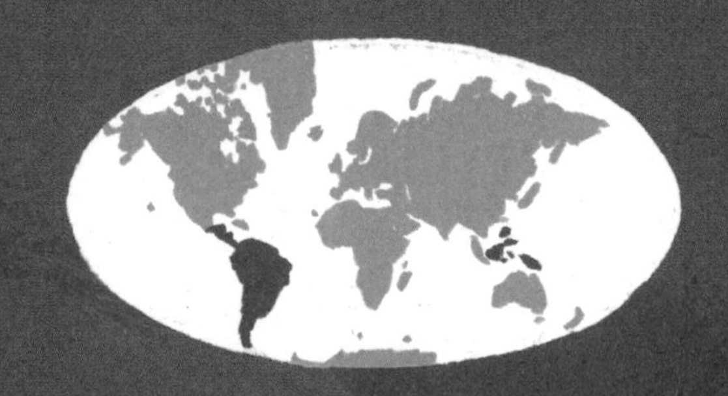

Terrain: Volcanoes, dormant and live

Sightings: Andes mountains, Galápagos Islands, Indonesia and South America

Colour: Black, purple or red

Size: 5 metres / 16 feet

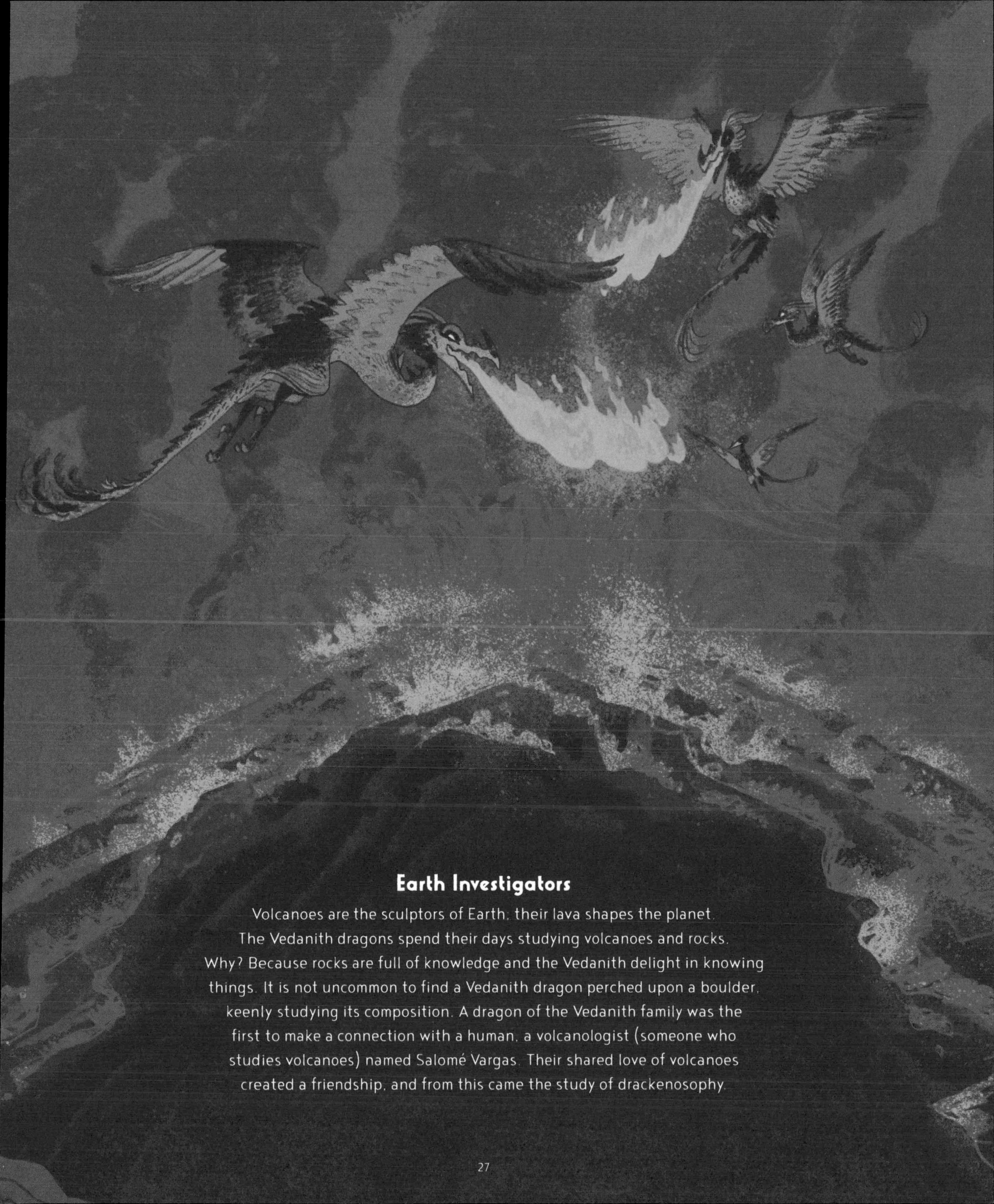

Earth Investigators

Volcanoes are the sculptors of Earth; their lava shapes the planet. The Vedanith dragons spend their days studying volcanoes and rocks. Why? Because rocks are full of knowledge and the Vedanith delight in knowing things. It is not uncommon to find a Vedanith dragon perched upon a boulder, keenly studying its composition. A dragon of the Vedanith family was the first to make a connection with a human, a volcanologist (someone who studies volcanoes) named Salomé Vargas. Their shared love of volcanoes created a friendship, and from this came the study of drackenosophy.

The Hasanas Family

The Hasanas are aquatic dragons that swim through seas and slide up estuaries, silent as a midnight thief. They have been spotted as far inland as a river will flow, although most prefer the salty seas. They wallow in pools and dip their multiple heads up and down as they swim. Along the banks of a muddy river, their heads camouflage well among the reeds. They are wingless, serpentine and the most cunning among dragons. In some parts of the world they are said to shape-shift, turning their several monstrous heads into one that resembles a human.

Terrain: Flooded forests, swamps and sea

Sightings: Greece, India, Scotland and Sri Lanka

Colour: Blue, green or teal

Size: 1-8 metres / 3-26 feet

Playful Pranksters

The Hasanas can have between two and a hundred heads. They are by far the most terrifying dragon to behold, but also the most playful. To be surrounded by a Hasanas is to find yourself facing many gleaming eyes, and feel the breath from many forked tongues. Beware of their tricks and their cunning smiles. There is a saying amongst the Hasanas: 'many heads make for good company!' These dragons are rarely lonely. One head can tell a joke while the others howl in laughter.

The Samaza Family

Tramp, thud, trundle and hiss. These are the dragons of dragon mist! The Samaza hide in forests of pine, birch, aspen and oak. Their lairs tunnel deep below the roots and into chambers below. Their scales glimmer green, red, yellow or brown to better hide among the trees, and their feet are flexible to scramble over the bark. The young often scuttle up the tree trunks in search of a bird's nest, or lie in wait along the branches, keeping an eye out for unsuspecting deer and rabbits.

Terrain: Aspen, birch, oak and pine forests

Sightings: England, Germany, Norway, Sweden, USA and Wales

Colour: Brown, green, red or yellow

Size: 7 metres / 22 feet

Hidden Hunters

The Samaza are shy, preferring to keep hidden by spraying a fine veil of dragon mist before creeping out of their lairs. The mist is belched out, leaving a distinct smell of burnt food in the murky air. These dragons lurk in the forests of Europe and North America. As their prey approaches, the horizon will suddenly disappear and the air will grow heavy as the dragon mist rolls between shrubs and trees. If one day you find yourself in a surrounding mist, keep your ears alert where your eyes fail you. The distinct rattle of scales nearby means that you've been spotted. You must only proceed on your current path with the greatest caution!

The Cittash Family

The Cittash are dragons of ice and snow, cold sea islands and jagged rock. Many make their lairs in the glowing blue of a glacier's innards. They slither through cracks called crevasses or sit atop an iceberg as the winds howl and whip through the air. The Cittash are the only dragons that hibernate in deep winter. They are also the only dragon with soft down on the underside of their scales, which can be puffed out to trap air and keep the body warm. Before winter descends, the Cittash hunt and eat more fish to keep them going through the darker months.

Terrain: Glaciers and tundras
Sightings: Canada, England, Greenland, Russia and Scotland
Colour: Light blue or white
Size: 9 metres / 30 feet

Dragon Song

Dash, dive, cower and hide! We sing our warning 'cross the tide.
Be you beastie large or small, we'll crush your bones so heed our call...

The Cittash's song can be heard drifting over the high winds of the tundra. They are highly protective dragons who can often be found perching on a cliff edge singing songs of warning to sailors drifting by. 'Do not spoil our land of ice,' they say. 'Do not dirty the waters for our fish,' they growl. Cittash dragons feel at home when near the sea, and they all love to fish in the waters around their lairs. If you keep a safe distance, you might glimpse one as they dive from an iceberg, searching for a tasty tuna or juicy octopus.

The Yukyuktakas Family

In the swelling heat of sun and sand, where the air blisters in the afternoon heat, the Yukyuktakas slumber on the ground. The weight of their body sinks into the sand with their wings splayed out around them. To the unobservant eye, it may look like nothing more than a rock or a dune. When the night chills the desert air, they stretch their creaking limbs and shake off heavy layers of sand. The darkness is when they snap up prey. Their eyes are as golden as their scales, and are sharp enough to allow the dragons to hunt at night.

Terrain: Arid mountains and deserts

Sightings: Australia, deserts of central Africa, Middle East and USA

Colour: Beige, gold, green or reddish brown

Size: 3 metres / 10 feet

Dragons of Lightning

The Yukyuktakas may look slow and sleepy, but don't be fooled by what you see. These are the dragons of lightning and thunder. The season of rain in the deserts is brought on by the magic in the Yukyuktakas' yearly dance. Every March they gather in swarms and as they dance, they call to the rain and thunder which sweeps across dry lands. On their nightly flights they swoop like nimble acrobats in the sky. You might hear their delighted cackle, a sound of 'yuk yuk!', as they glide and dive.

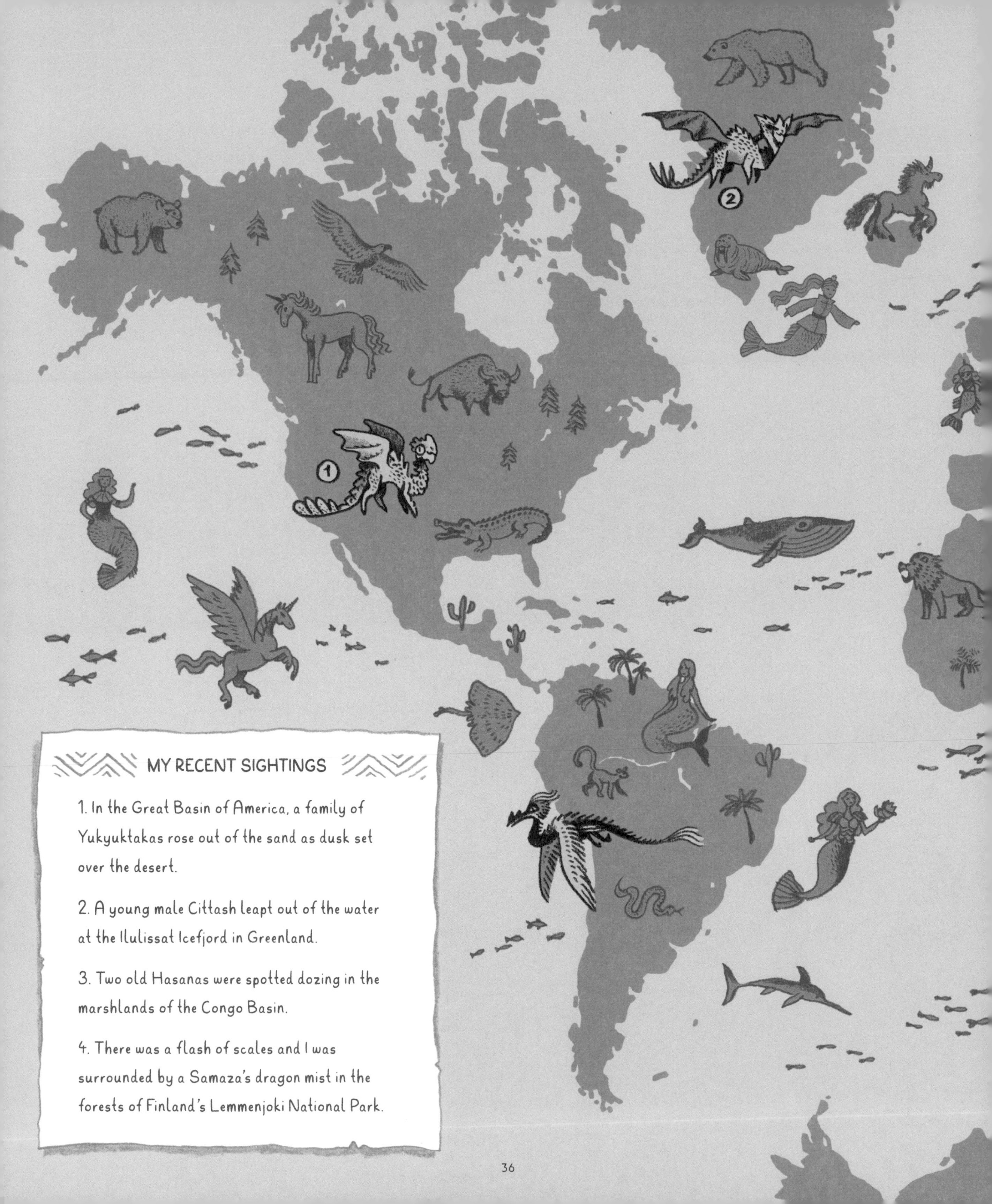

MY RECENT SIGHTINGS

1. In the Great Basin of America, a family of Yukyuktakas rose out of the sand as dusk set over the desert.

2. A young male Cittash leapt out of the water at the Ilulissat Icefjord in Greenland.

3. Two old Hasanas were spotted dozing in the marshlands of the Congo Basin.

4. There was a flash of scales and I was surrounded by a Samaza's dragon mist in the forests of Finland's Lemmenjoki National Park.

Dragon Sightings

As a professor of drackenosophy, I've been lucky enough to travel to all corners of the world to discover dragons in the wild. On this map, I have noted some of the sightings I've made on my voyages and with a bit of good fortune, it could help young drackenosophers spot some too.

Part III
ANCIENT DRAGON HISTORY

Once, a very long time ago, there was a great kingdom of dragons. We know parts of their stories from the myths of the human world. Our memory of dragons goes all the way back to the people of Ancient Sumer, 5,000 years ago. Over many years more stories appeared, like the dragon in India who could hold monsoon waters in its belly. Or the Norse Viking story of Nidhogga, a dragon of death that chewed on the roots of Yggdrasil, the tree of life. Many know of the red dragon of Wales who battled against the white dragon to show Welsh strength.

Dragons have played their role in human history, but what about the history of dragons? Here we learn briefly of famous dragons, and the famous dragon slayers. Then we will unearth true dragon history and culture, the colourful lives of dragons, and why they have become so scarce in our world today...

Famous Dragons

Dragons appear in countless stories and accounts from all corners of the world. These dragons have frightened and fascinated the people that have lived near and around their lairs. A few of these are still remembered today, and are studied by drackenosophers analysing dragon history.

Vritra: The Hindu Dragon

Vritra was a powerful dragon: so large his yawning mouth could swallow chunks of the night sky. His whiskers were the colour of copper and his torso towered black and tall. He could stop rivers and lakes from flowing, and block out the sun with his body. Men, women and gods feared Vritra's power. In his final battle against Indra the Thunder God, Vritra swallowed his enemy whole. But the Thunder God released himself by cutting the soft belly from the inside and striking Vritra with a deadly thunder bolt. The story of Vritra is told in one of the greatest Hindu epic stories of all time, the *Mahabharata*.

Lung Wang: Ancient China

Lung Wang was the Dragon King who lived in a crystal palace under the sea with his four brother dragons. He was a life-giving dragon, guardian of the weather and seas, protector of sailors. He was horned and whiskered with a curled beard of wisdom. Like many dragons across China, he was loved and worshipped for being kind to the people. Lung Wang is remembered with sculptures and dances, and he is celebrated in the Lunar New Year.

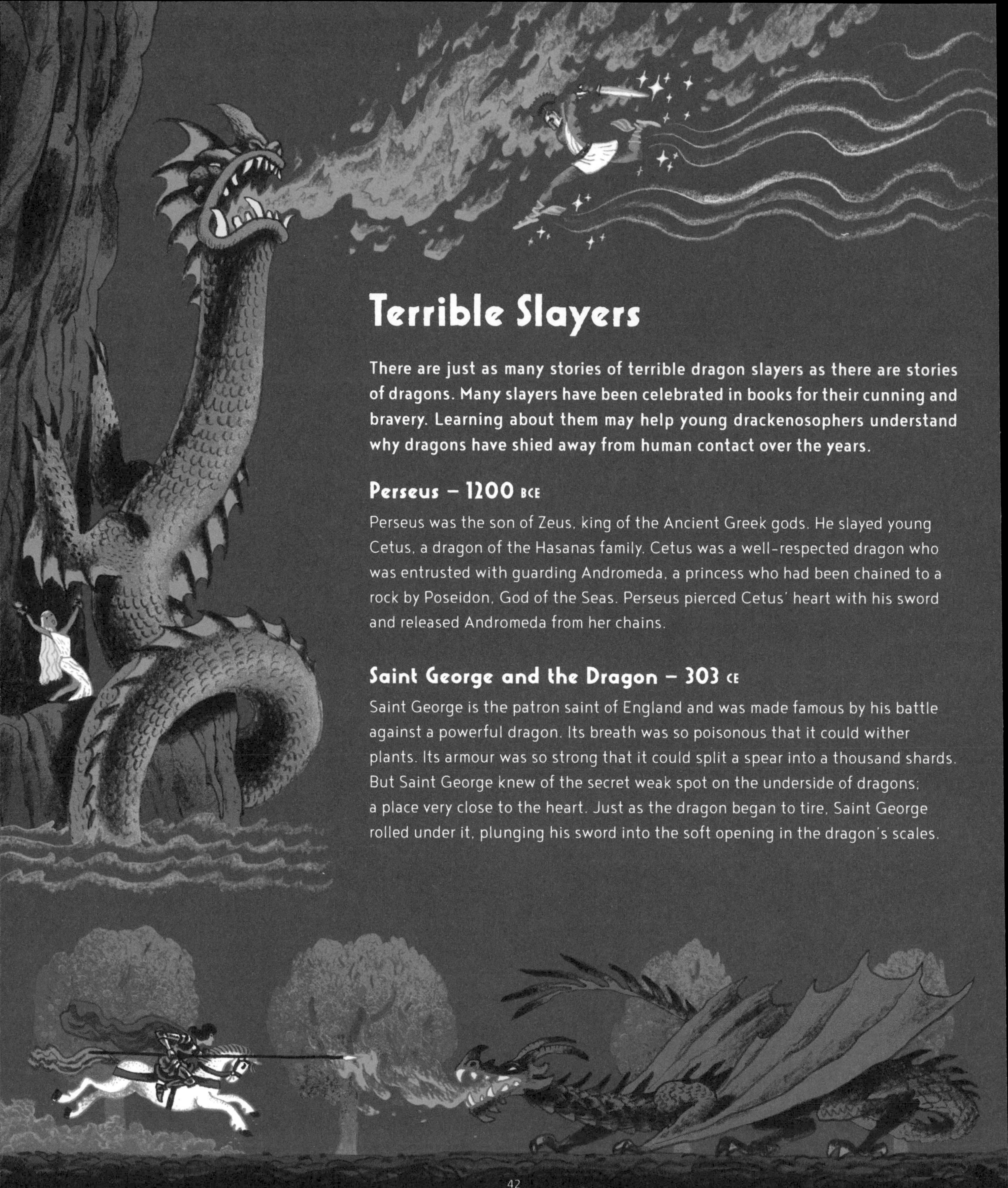

Terrible Slayers

There are just as many stories of terrible dragon slayers as there are stories of dragons. Many slayers have been celebrated in books for their cunning and bravery. Learning about them may help young drackenosophers understand why dragons have shied away from human contact over the years.

Perseus – 1200 BCE

Perseus was the son of Zeus, king of the Ancient Greek gods. He slayed young Cetus, a dragon of the Hasanas family. Cetus was a well-respected dragon who was entrusted with guarding Andromeda, a princess who had been chained to a rock by Poseidon, God of the Seas. Perseus pierced Cetus' heart with his sword and released Andromeda from her chains.

Saint George and the Dragon – 303 CE

Saint George is the patron saint of England and was made famous by his battle against a powerful dragon. Its breath was so poisonous that it could wither plants. Its armour was so strong that it could split a spear into a thousand shards. But Saint George knew of the secret weak spot on the underside of dragons; a place very close to the heart. Just as the dragon began to tire, Saint George rolled under it, plunging his sword into the soft opening in the dragon's scales.

Beowulf – 510 CE

Beowulf was a fierce Swedish warrior, eventually crowned king. After an old Samaza dragon occupied some of his land, he tracked her to her lair, slipping silently through the entrance and catching her by surprise. Panicked, she blew fire wildly through the mountain so that their battle took place among the flames. As the King struck the dragon's scales, he broke his sword in two, and the dragon dealt him a deadly blow to the neck. Before he died, Beowulf's knife found purchase in the dragon's side and both perished that day.

Siegfried – 1030 CE

Siegfried was a warrior who killed Fafnir, a Cittash dragon and guardian of a magic treasure hoard. Fafnir's story was first written in the Icelandic stories called the *Volsungs Sagas*. They tell of Fafnir's treasures including an enchanted helmet, a golden coat of chainmail and a sword called Ridill. After killing Fafnir, Siegfried bathed in the dragon's blood, coating himself with the magic of immortality that ran from the wound.

The Last Kingdom of Dragons

For almost 10,000 years, dragons lived together in the Last Kingdom. At the centre of the kingdom lay the City of Fire, a magnificent society just for dragons. Here thousands of different dragons lived together in burnt tunnels that connected the city and formed a network in mountains and sea caves. They excavated marvellous rooms, dug out and stored precious stones, sang dragon songs and danced on the winds of the world.

Inside the City of Fire

The City of Fire was expertly built, home to the best dragon construction in history. There was the Stadium of Play, where the fittest dragons competed in games. The Chamber of Songs was carved so precisely that even a whisper would bounce like a roar off the walls. There was also the Vaults of Many, a dragon treasury that funnelled deep below the city's tallest mountain. Hundreds of dragons worked there, counting and studying the treasure, keeping it safe.

The Meeting Place

The Council of Dragons was a group of elders who made important decisions about dragon safety. In 1561, they met on a mountain of crystal and glass to discuss the threat of humans to dragonkind. Above the roaring winds, each dragon took their turn to speak. It was here that they made the decision to abandon the Last Kingdom, and live far from human sight. Before they left, they pounded the entrances into the ground and made sure that the gateways had crumbled completely. They blocked off the tunnels that led to the City of Fire, and finally they fled, never to live in great numbers again. Drackenosophers are still searching for the remains of the Last Kingdom and the City of Fire to this day.

A Dragon's Home

A dragon's home is called a lair. Dragons spend a lot of time in their lairs, and they take great pride in them. Lairs are always well hidden within earth, rock or ice where it is pleasantly cool. The entrances are small and concealed, but lairs are surprisingly spacious once inside the inner rooms. So far, three types of lair have been identified: caves, mounds and below water.

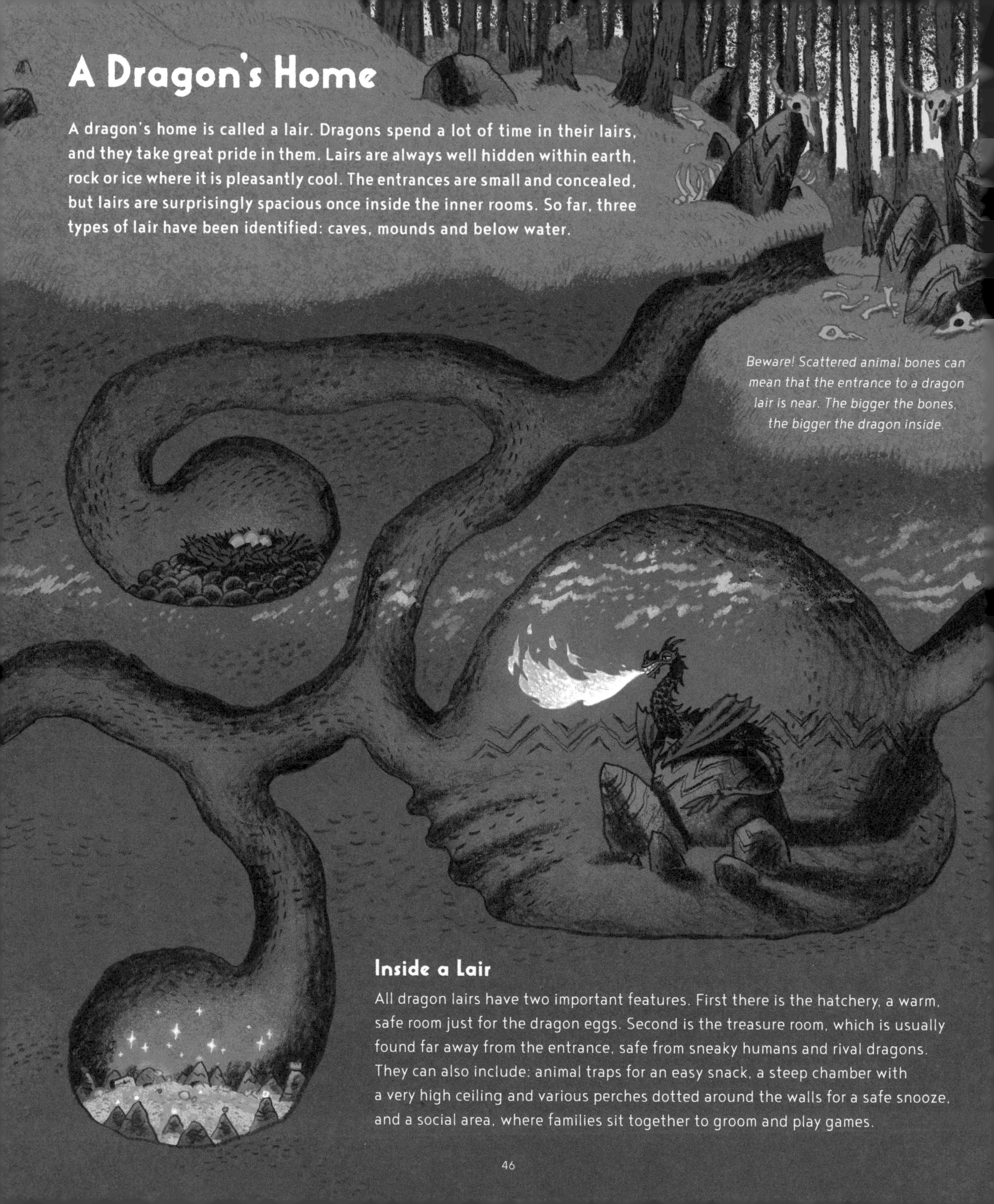

Beware! Scattered animal bones can mean that the entrance to a dragon lair is near. The bigger the bones, the bigger the dragon inside.

Inside a Lair

All dragon lairs have two important features. First there is the hatchery, a warm, safe room just for the dragon eggs. Second is the treasure room, which is usually found far away from the entrance, safe from sneaky humans and rival dragons. They can also include: animal traps for an easy snack, a steep chamber with a very high ceiling and various perches dotted around the walls for a safe snooze, and a social area, where families sit together to groom and play games.

Caves

Cracks in mountains and volcanoes are often cleared out to make a cave lair. Dragons burn through the rock and scratch away to make tunnels which curl and twist into a mountain's heart. These are often very deep and cool inside. If you venture near a mountain cave, you can be sure it's a dragon's doorway.

Mounds

Some lairs stick out of the ground. From an earthen mound in the forest, to sand dunes on beaches or in the desert, they have an opening at their base that is covered up with carefully arranged boulders. To the untrained eye, it might simply resemble an animal's burrow or a neat collection of rocks. Drackenosophers keep an eye out for sticks and rocks that look suspiciously well-organised.

Below Water

These vast, deep lairs are mostly found under seas or lakes. They are accessible via an underwater cave or an opening that has been dug out from the water's edge so that air can reach down into the dark and damp caverns. Dragons living in underwater lairs will often create pool chambers by allowing the water to drip from the ceiling above, creating a natural dragon bath.

Treasure

It is true that dragons love treasure. They adore all that shimmers, they're dazzled by diamonds and purr just at the thought of gold. They tend to their treasures, keeping them safe under watchful eyes. But treasure to a dragon is not about riches, it is the feel and touch of something rare from the earth. A dragon will look deep into a ruby to see how it was formed. It will sift gold through its claws to hear it tinkle. This has earned them a bad reputation among humans who would often like the treasure for themselves.

Agate:
To ward off danger in perilous times

Quartz:
Popular with water dragons

Iron:
Polished to make jewellery

Pearl:
Given to a baby dragon when it hatches

Treasure and Tradition

Throughout dragon history, collecting precious items has been an important activity. Dragons have always traded gems and sparkling stones as tokens of goodwill. It was a way of forming friendships and showing that no harm was meant. Nowadays, older dragons hand down their favourite pieces to wish young dragons luck when they leave home.

The Smuggler's Trove

The Smuggler's Trove is a treasure hoard collected by a notorious dragon called Shia the Shadow. She could pick her way into a high-security safe without leaving a wisp. Shia's collection was filled with magnificent pieces swiped from Incan emperors and Aztec empresses, from the Crown Jewels of England and even the buried tombs of the Ancient Egyptians. When the City of Fire was abandoned, Shia pilfered the most precious pieces and added them to her collection. The Smuggler's Trove has never been found...

Language

Dragon language is much older than human language, and there are very few written examples of it. Every story and historical event is memorised and passed down from dragon to dragon verbally. Young dragons first learn about how to be thoughtful dragons through their bedtime stories, and as adults they share tales, riddles and even jokes! Dragons can communicate with humans if they choose to, but it is not easy for a human to speak Dragon. Their words can flick between soft sounds formed on their forked tongues, to an ear-splitting growl.

Dragon Riddles:*

1. I am a bridge without water, I wrinkle but not with time. What am I?

2. I can touch the sky and burrow deep below the sea. My head is smaller than my feet. I am strong against strength but can be weathered weak. What am I?

3. What goes up but never comes back down?

Simple Phrases

Try pronouncing some simple phrases yourself, and then perhaps teach your friends and family the ways of dragon speech:

DRAGON	ENGLISH
Hak oom darsh y shong?	Is your day going well?
Hak tojok zu prath?	Is there food nearby?
Sog oos rach toos thieyst?	What can you see?
Nang ko toos	Thank you
Hoyoth	Yes
Donjath	No

*Answers to riddles: 1. A nose 2. A mountain 3. Your age

Dragon Song

Dragons delight in singing. Dragon song is made up of a very similar structure to poetry. Each line has a beat, called a metre, and when they sing in this way it makes a wonderful rhythm. There are songs of old stories, and others which depict a mood, like sadness or excitement, or the readiness to be friends. When a chorus of dragons sing together, the band will thump and drum their tails and tap their claws along their scales to keep time and add rhythm.

Part IV
DRACKENOSOPHY

Drackenosophy began in 1393 with a research paper titled 'Research Notes on Dragons'. The researcher, Salomé Vargas, founded a small school, which in turn became a global network of schools all under the name the 'World School of Dragons'. As the WSoD produced more and more talented drackenosophers, the way people saw dragons began to change, so that today they are no longer viewed as monsters, but as sweet creatures, full of personality and good humour.

The World School of Dragons has a growing number of dedicated students. With improved technology, we now have heatproof materials, oxygen tanks and advanced recording equipment to get closer to dragons in the wild. The most important work for drackenosophers is to conserve the wild spaces that dragons live in. From replanting destroyed forests to fishing carefully around their water lairs, in this chapter you will learn more about what it takes to become a good drackenosopher, so grab your notebook and fireproof jacket, and let's begin...

Dragon Watching

Dragon watching is not an easy task. They are elusive creatures and most work very hard to keep the location of their lairs a secret. A drackenosopher that is courageous enough to go dragon watching must follow careful instructions and pack wisely for the quest. It can be a back-breaking task of sweat, nerves and patience! But the rewards are better than you could ever dream of.

A Drackenosopher's Pack:

- Heatproof gloves
- Pen, paper and drawing materials (preferably in a fireproof container)
- A hat or scarf to cover your head
- A book of riddles and jokes
- Any musical instrument (singing can soothe tricky situations with some dragons)

Common Mistakes

There have been many unfortunate accidents among drackenosophers, some of which could have been easily avoided. Drackenosophers have now learnt that it is unwise to approach a dragon youngling. Small and innocent as they may seem, there will be family nearby. Leave jewellery and anything sparkly at home, unless you do not mind losing it (clothes included). Do not linger too close to a dragon's tail as it could accidentally flick and injure you, and avoid staring directly into a dragon's eyes unless you want to offend it.

Dragon Watching Secrets

Each drackenosopher has their own methods for watching and tracking dragons. Yet there are a few known tricks among us which can be shared, such as scanning the horizon to catch them in slow and graceful flight. Or watching when birds gather near the water, in case we spot a snap of jaws from underneath to claim an easy dinner. Or simply listening carefully for the flap of leathery wings, the sliding rustle of belly on earth, or even faint dragon song on the breeze.

The Hall of Drackenosophers

Painted, photographed, hung up and framed. These are the portraits of our most famous drackenosophers! They were pioneers in the field, clever in their endeavours and famous for their work and discoveries.

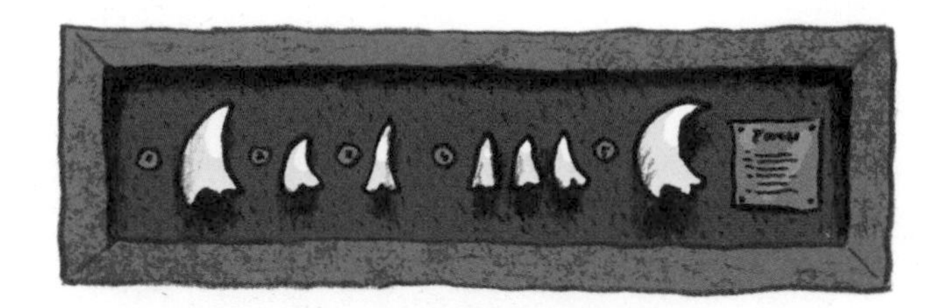

Alwin Jones 1484–1519

Alwin was an expert at the science of the pen! He could draw with absolute precision. Alwin's technical and anatomical drawings in observation helped us understand a dragon's anatomy and capture the exquisite beauty of dragons around the world.

Salomé Vargas 1368–1446

The founder of the World School of Dragons in 1383 at the bright age of 25. Salomé befriended a young dragon whilst researching rocks near the Coropuna Volcano. She became the first human to learn about dragon history and social orders. Her first paper, 'Research Notes on Dragons', became the core philosophy of drackenosophy.

Aditi Roy 1915–1984

Aditi was famed for her playful wit, clear logic and sharp tongue. She encountered many Hasanas near her home in India, gaining much respect among them for her intellect. Aditi persuaded the dragons to reveal the meaning of their words, and in return she shared new human words, jokes and riddles.

Kandisiko Kataparo 1931–2004

Kandisiko was famed for re-introducing wild dragons into the north of Namibia. As the young dragons grew, she observed their development and recorded their behaviour. Her protective nature earned her the name 'Dragon Defender' among the Yukyuktakas.

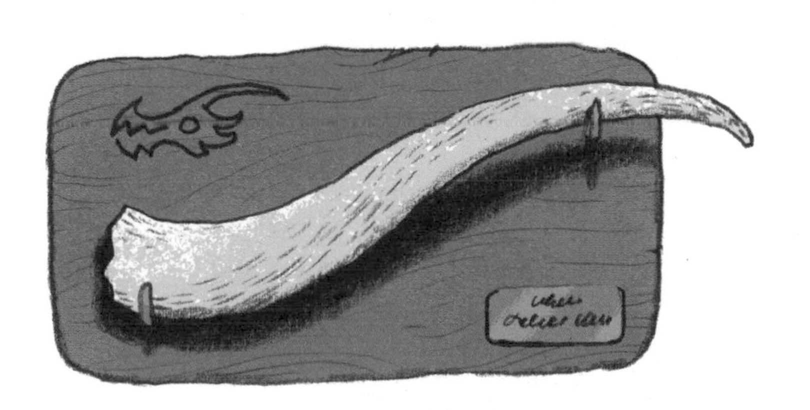

The World School of Dragons

Hidden within all great cities, there is a building with winding corridors and polished walls containing students of drackenosophy. The WSoD is made up of many schools across the globe which collect ancient texts in their vaults, send out missions to investigate dragons in their area and analyse data gathered on expeditions. They work in partnership to write accurate guides and papers on dragons to keep the history and study of dragons alive.

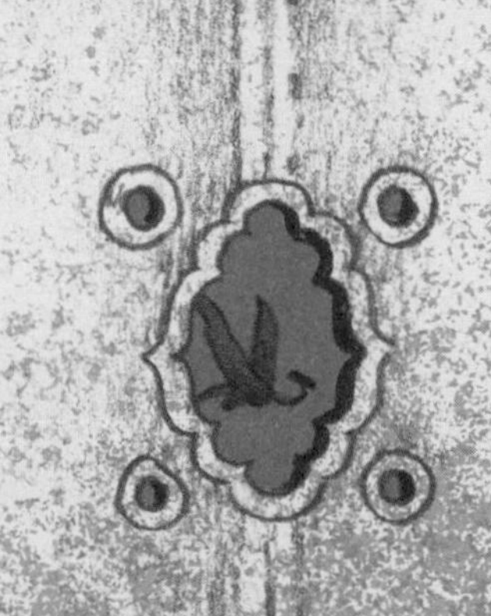

Breakthroughs

By working together, students have been making incredible progress. An exciting breakthrough by students in Delhi has led to the creation of a Smoke Capture Canvas. This clever contraption collects a dragon's smoke patterns and transfers the amazing shapes in perfect form onto the canvas. Dragon art will soon be in galleries everywhere!

Flying Professor

Most dragons keep to themselves in the wild, but through the history of the WSoD there have been curious and willing dragons who have joined professors to teach dragon history. They do not live in the cities but journey in to give a guest lecture every now and again. For example, the WSoD in London hosts an ancient dragon named Roya Elda, a fantastically intelligent figure who teaches the 'Gold Appreciation and Curation' course.

Continuing the Journey

Dragons have existed on Earth for as long as human memory, and they will continue for just as long. Their survival has not come from their strength or power; it comes from listening to what the Earth's winds tell them, from finding truth in the rocks and being brave and wise in times of trouble. Dragons all know one thing above all: if the winds buffet against you and the rain quells your fire, think of why it does so and work to make things better. Take the courage you have and go and learn some more...

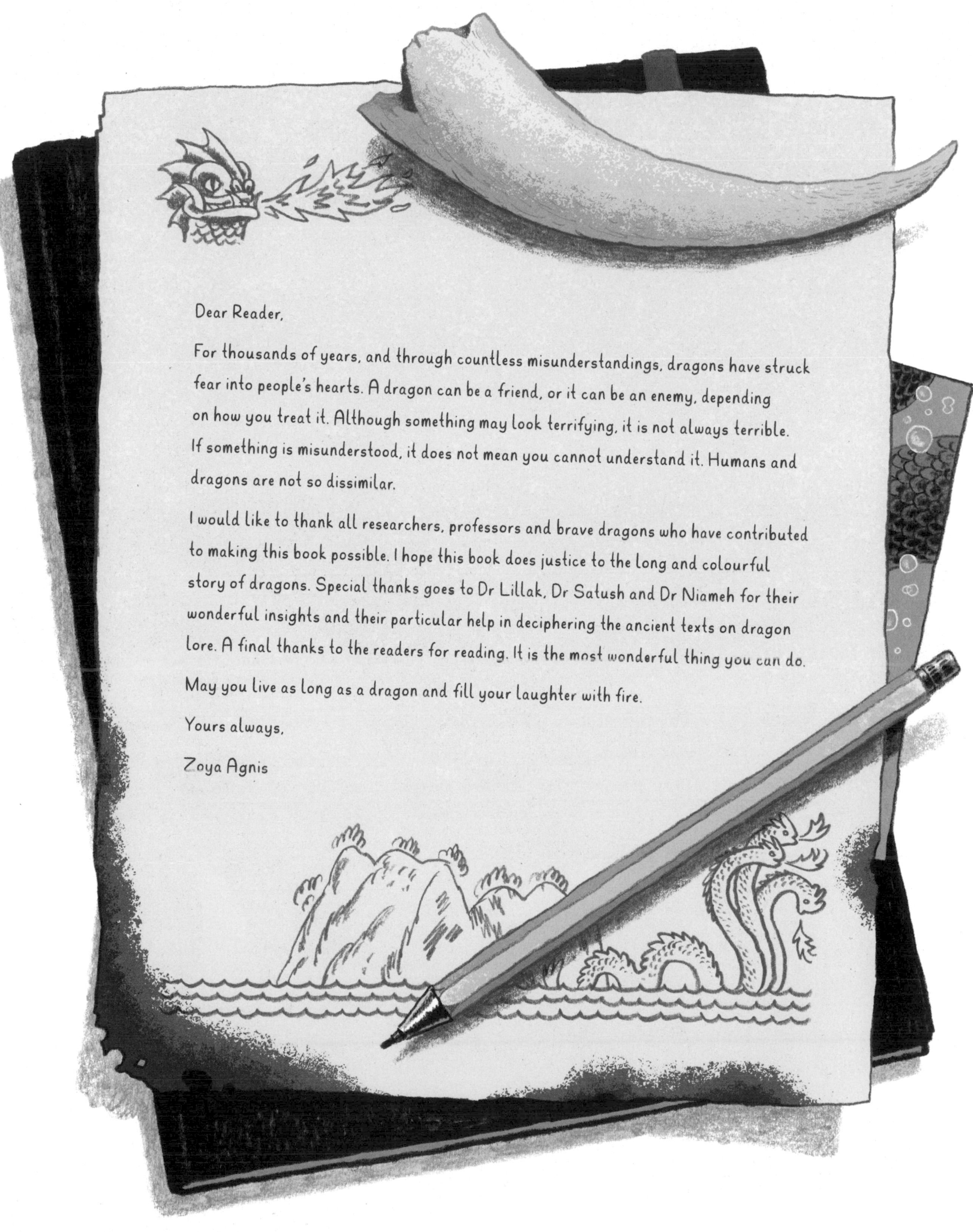

Dear Reader,

For thousands of years, and through countless misunderstandings, dragons have struck fear into people's hearts. A dragon can be a friend, or it can be an enemy, depending on how you treat it. Although something may look terrifying, it is not always terrible. If something is misunderstood, it does not mean you cannot understand it. Humans and dragons are not so dissimilar.

I would like to thank all researchers, professors and brave dragons who have contributed to making this book possible. I hope this book does justice to the long and colourful story of dragons. Special thanks goes to Dr Lillak, Dr Satush and Dr Niameh for their wonderful insights and their particular help in deciphering the ancient texts on dragon lore. A final thanks to the readers for reading. It is the most wonderful thing you can do.

May you live as long as a dragon and fill your laughter with fire.

Yours always,

Zoya Agnis

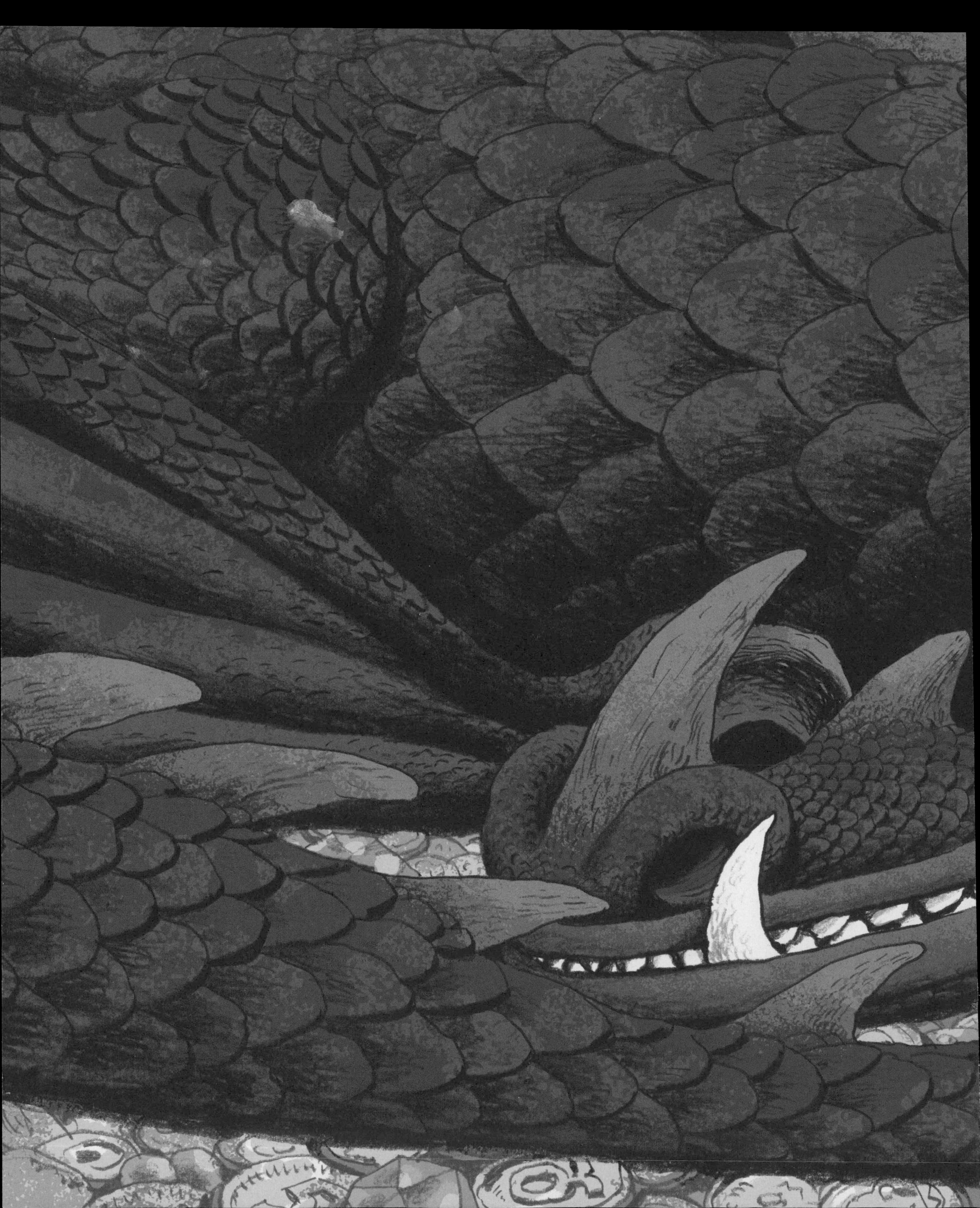